For Jack, my tiny bookworm,
this one's for you—
A. H.

In memory of Paul Shobbrook,
who shaped my career in so many ways—
T. W.

tiger tales
5 River Road, Suite 128, Wilton, CT 06897
Published in the United States 2022
Published in Great Britain 2022
by Little Tiger Press Ltd.
First published in Germany 2021
Text by Amelia Hepworth
Text copyright © 2021 Little Tiger Press Ltd.
Illustrations copyright © 2021 Tim Warnes
Visit Tim Warnes at www.TimWarnes.com
ISBN-13: 978-1-68010-260-4
ISBN-10: 1-68010-260-5
Printed in China
LTP/2800/4074/0721

10 9 8 7 6 5 4 3 2 1

www.tigertalesbooks.com

The Forest Stewardship Council® (FSC®) is an international,
non-governmental organization dedicated to promoting responsible
management of the world's forests. FSC® operates a system of forest
certification and product labeling that allows consumers to identify
wood and wood-based products from well-managed forests.

For more information about the FSC®, please visit their website at www.fsc.org

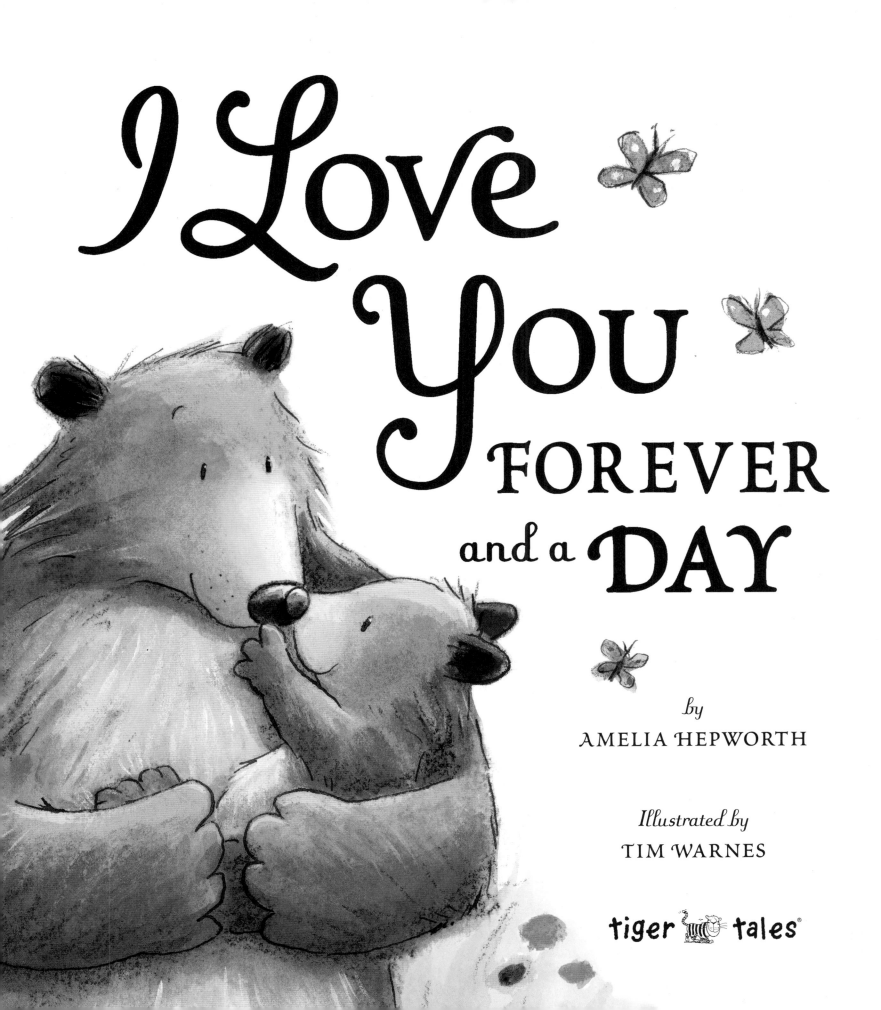

I Love You FOREVER and a DAY

by
AMELIA HEPWORTH

Illustrated by
TIM WARNES

tiger tales

If I could imagine
a day just for you,

The sun would be shining;
the sky would be blue.

I would tell you a story;
   I would sing you a song . . . .

With your hand in mine,
we would hop-skip along.

I would tell you
the best thing is
watching you grow;

I would tell you I'm with you wherever you go.

We would gather a rainbow to brighten the sky;

We would splash in the river –
you would leap from up high.

And when the sun sets
on our magical day,

I would gather you up as your sleepy legs sway.

The stars in the night sky
would guide us to bed,
and on our way home,
I would kiss your soft head.

We'd snuggle together,
and gently I'd say
I love you, my small one –
forever and a day.